BOSSY HUCOW MÉNAGE

Dark BDSM Fertile Story

Leandra Camilli

CONTENTS

Title Page

Copyright

Chapter 1   1

Chapter 2   4

Chapter 3   8

Chapter 4   11

Chapter 5   15

Chapter 6   18

Epilogue   21

Similar Books   23

About the Author   25

CHAPTER 1

I felt like I was trapped. Trapped with this guy, who didn't know what to do with me. We were sitting on the couch, watching something on TV. What were we watching? I couldn't even pay attention to what the screen was displaying.

And despite him making me think that I was wasting my time, I couldn't help but sneak my hand under his pants and look for his cock.

"Warren, you are my boyfriend, so you better make me think that this is worth it."

He turned his head to look at me and there was something different in his eyes. Even though what I had just said was a little more direct than what I usually said when we were having some sexy time, he still didn't try to rebuke me.

For now, he was just looking at me and probably thinking about how pitiful he was. I would never hide that about him. He was like that and there wasn't much he could do about it other than feel humiliated.

At least his cock was a little bit bigger than the average size, but it was still not enough for me. Every time that I thought about it, I found myself wanting a massive, oversized prick to grip with my hand. And I could already imagine myself sliding my hand on it, devouring it.

Would that ever happen? I didn't think so. I wasn't holding my breath for it.

"Sorry, love. It's just the way I am and I think that you should have known that things are this way with me. If anything, you should be more open-minded about who I am."

I groaned, putting my hand around his cock and beginning to stroke it. We were alone in my room, but I was wishing we were in a public space, like a subway car so that everybody could see how slutty I was. I was like that and I didn't hide that from anybody.

"You're making me so disappointed in being your girlfriend, and that's something I thought I would never say," I said before increasing the speed of my hand and now it was going up and down, making Warren even harder than he was already. He had thought that was impossible, I could tell just by looking at his eyes.

Then, I glanced down, finding his prick, which was already outside of his pants. After that, I began to fondle his balls, and I could tell that he was already on the verge of having a climax.

When it happened, it would wash over his entire body and he would most likely pass out, just like it happened so many times when I thought we were going to have sex.

Another reason why I thought he was a puny, worthless man was the fact that he didn't want to fuck me properly and take my virginity.

My pussy was begging for a proper man to do that and I could only wonder when the right opportunity to accomplish that was going to present itself.

A few seconds after that and Warren exploded in my hand, shooting out rope after rope of his come all over his belly, which was another reason why this was disappointing.

I wanted him doing this either in my mouth or in my pussy. I wanted him splitting me open and cumming in there, breeding me with his heir.

My mouth was already salivating just thinking about that.

Alas, it wasn't going to happen – at least, not tonight. After he finished cumming on my hand, he shut his eyes and didn't open them again. And he was even already snoring and showing me that he wasn't interested in anything else tonight.

All in all, this was as disappointing as I thought it was going to be and one of the reasons why we had to break up right now.

I kissed him on his cheek and said, "Warren, I think that I'm going to break up with you. My life is boring enough working as a secretary for those millionaires, and I think that I want to take Mr. Leach up on his offer. I want him to turn me into a hucow and you are okay with that, right?"

I checked his eyes and… Yeah. I knew that he didn't have anything to say about that and even though he would miss me a lot after finding out that I was now living there with them, he could shove his worry about me up his ass.

Anyway, now I had to wipe my hand and clean it. I did that and then I took off my clothes, going to the bathroom. I needed to take a shower.

After doing that, I imagined Jeremy exploring my body with his hands, feeling every part of me. I imagined him stuffing me full with his dick and breeding me with his heir. And while doing that, I couldn't hold back the climax that surged in me, and it was devastating in a way that I never thought possible.

My body was even shaking and trembling, something that Warren could never replicate with me. That was how powerful my crush on Jeremy was.

Mr. Bleach. I imagined myself saying his name loudly while riding on his prick until he filled me with his thick, viscous cum.

My body was still feeling the aftershocks of that amazing orgasm, and that wasn't something that happened often. That was just how strong my need for Jeremy was.

Alright, it was decided. Tonight. No, *right now* I was going to call him and tell him the good news. Then, perhaps he would come to pick me up right here in my house instead of making me wait.

I never liked waiting.

CHAPTER 2

But he was making me wait. I was outside of my home and Warren was doing everything in his power to make me change my mind, but it wasn't going to work like that.

I pushed him away from me with my hand. "Warren, no matter how much you insist, I'm not going to change my mind. I'm going to the Dairy Club and I'm going to become their hucow. If you want, you can watch us as we have fun, but other than that, there isn't much you can do."

His eyes were still wide and he blinked several times in a row as if he was trying to understand what I said. After he realized that he was only wasting his time right now, he straightened up his spine and said, "alright, then I'm going with you, but only to make sure…"

"You want to be sure about what?" I asked, curious about what he was thinking. What was he thinking was going to happen when we were having fun and Jeremy was pounding in and out of me without mercy?

He was crazy if he was thinking that he could stop me from cheating on him. To be honest, I was only asking myself why it took me so long to make this decision.

A few seconds later, when Warren was opening his mouth again to ask me whatever else he thought he still needed to ask me, a limousine pulled over in front of me, and I knew that was Jeremy.

His window rolled down, revealing him. I opened a big smile

and the driver opened the door for me. I found myself with Jeremy sitting by my side. After Warren tried to get into the limousine, Jeremy put his hand against his chest, stopping him.

"I don't know what you think you're doing, but you are not allowed inside. Diana told me everything about what was going on with you and she doesn't want to be with you anymore. It's as simple as that."

Warren opened his mouth and for a moment I really thought that he was going to grow a pair, but then he shook his head and started to walk away.

I decided that I wasn't going to waste the opportunity to make him see everything, so I grabbed his hand and made him fall onto the seat, sitting by my other side.

Jeremy couldn't help but widen his eyes, asking me what I thought I was doing. "Trust me on this. With Warren around, the humiliation will be even more tempting and delicious. My pussy is already wet just thinking about it."

He licked his lips. "Your pussy is already like that? Wanna show me?" He asked, his eyes flashing with evilness.

I lowered my hand and put it under my pair of pants, dipping it into the wetness between my legs. Then, I took it out of there and showed it to him, nearing it to his nose.

He lowered his head, taking a good, long whiff. Then, he smirked, saying, "Ohh, Jesus. After smelling it, I feel like devouring you right now. I feel like I shouldn't even wait until Robert is with us. You really know how to tempt a man like me."

I smiled, looking at Warren, who couldn't stop blinking. What was he so surprised about?

I couldn't care less about what he was thinking right now, so I just decided to ignore him for the time being. I was also wet for something else, that being Jeremy's monster cock, and I was thinking that I couldn't wait until we were in his estate to have a little fun.

It was for that reason that I put my hand on his bulge and began to massage it, applying pressure on it at regular intervals. His eyes flashed with evilness again and he breathed heavily, putting his hand under my boob.

I could feel his hand applying pressure on it slowly and carefully. He knew what he was doing, and that wasn't surprising.

I moaned and put my fingers around his cock, stroking it, all the while relishing the fact that this was all happening while my former boyfriend could see every detail. And he was still so dumbfounded by all this that he couldn't do anything.

He couldn't fight back.

And just like so many times before this, I ignored him, letting out another moan of pleasure through my lips the moment I knew my orgasm was coming, and it was even better than I thought, one of the reasons why I sped up my hand, shooting it up and down his prick.

He was going to make me come as much as I was going to do the same to him.

By now, the limousine was already driving and I knew that we didn't have much time until we reached his estate. When we got there, Robert would surely smell that something happened, but he wouldn't be able to do anything.

And that was another reason why this spiced things up, my breathing accelerating. And then, it happened, my body trembling while he still fondled and massaged my boobs. I swear, it was as if he couldn't stop this even if he wanted to.

A moment after that, Jeremy exploded in my hand and coated it with his milk, making it wet. It was just as I thought it was going to be. It was mind-shattering and even after it was over, I could still feel the aftershocks of the amazing orgasm that he rewarded me with, and even though I couldn't know this for sure, I could still see that he thought the same way.

He moved his hand off my boob, saying, "that was amazing and I want to do it again with you. I want to do it after you've transformed. I feel that, after that, it will be even more rewarding than it was tonight, don't you think?"

And after he asked me that, I could only wonder if what he was proposing was going to happen tonight as well.

I couldn't help but hope that that was exactly what was going to happen.

CHAPTER 3

I opened my eyes and found myself lying on the bed, wondering where Jeremy was. He said that as soon as the transformation was over, he was going to be by my side and give me a lot of pleasure.

I licked my lips, thinking about that. Was it going to take him too long to show up?

The room was dark and I couldn't see much. This was so infuriating, I thought after some seconds filled with waiting and more of the same. Even though I couldn't say this for sure, I was beginning to think that he fooled me when he said that he was going to be around here waiting for my transformation to finish.

And it did finish. I didn't need to look at myself in the mirror to know that.

I stood up and began to walk around the room, looking for the light switch, and struggling with doing that. I didn't know what was going on, but it felt like the switch was nowhere to be found, which was annoying.

"Dammit, where the fuck is it?" I asked myself, in a moment feeling a hand landing on my shoulder and, after gasping, I realized that the person behind me was none other than... Robert! I hadn't seen him after coming here, and this entire time I had been asking myself where he was.

"Robert?" I asked. I had seen his face before, so I recognized it immediately after seeing him.

The most surprising thing about this was that he had been

in the same room with me the entire time. One other surprising thing about this was that he was naked from top to bottom, and his body was even more delicious than Jeremy's.

To be honest, fuck Jeremy. He made me wait this entire time to see if he was going to come and fuck me, and now I was with someone that was going to fill in the gap left by him.

"That's right, pretty. It's me."

"Have you been watching me sleep this entire time?" I asked. I had to go straight to the point with that, and he wasn't fazed by my question.

"No, of course not," he gave me a devilish smile. "I would never do something like that. In fact, I was only waiting for you to wake up. I want to fuck you right now and I think that you want the same, don't you?"

Right after saying that, he put his fingers around his dick, and I couldn't help but wonder if he was even bigger than Jeremy.

I also couldn't stop licking my lips, and I supposed that was something that was going to be happening a lot more often from now on.

"Everything you want to do to me, Master. I want you to fuck me, but there is a condition."

"Oh, there is? You are feeling pretty bossy right now, aren't you?"

He began to pump his shaft slowly, enticing me to go down on my knees in front of him and suck him off. To be honest, I was only wondering when he was going to ask me to do that. My mind was already obsessing over the idea of making that real.

To feel his massive dong filling my mouth with everything that he had, and then he would even feed me with his semen. I just felt overwhelmed by the possibility of that happening.

"Yeah, there's that condition and I think that you should respect it."

He guffawed.

"You really are different from the other members we have here, which is one of the reasons why I think that we are going to get along just fine." I opened my mouth, but then he added, "and

I think that we should go where I can brand you. Don't worry, it won't take long. Jeremy has already left the rod heated, after all."

He was really going to brand me? It wasn't enough that I was transformed into his hucow, he was also going to make sure that anybody else that saw me knew that I was his. Theirs. A member of the Dairy Club.

I already felt shivers running down my spine just hearing that.

He took me outside of his house and then he brought the heated rod, asking me to go down on all fours, which I did. Following that, he pressed the end of the heated rod to my butt, which was the region where everybody could see the mark. It was a welt that could never be removed and that thought already made the hair on my skin shoot up.

I was his and nothing and no one would change that, I thought with a smile on my face. After that, he went behind me and settled his hands on my ass, kneeling behind me. I couldn't help but wonder what he was going to do, and I was nicely surprised when he began to massage it.

After a while, I started to wish he was fondling my boobs. They were already aching to be milked, one of the reasons why they were already leaking.

And as if he could read my mind, Robert leaned over, putting his mouth close to my ear. "Don't worry, pretty. I'm going to milk you when the time is right. For now, I'm preparing you for something naughty that I'm planning on doing to you."

Something naughty that he was planning to do to me? I couldn't help but wonder what that was, but I didn't have much time to think about that, considering that he just took something in his hand, and then, without any other preparation, he slid something into my ass.

And I had to wonder what it was.

CHAPTER 4

Robert slid his hand over the back of my neck, saying, "it's a butt plug, silly. What did you think it was?"

I moaned and... mooed. That was right. I mooed and it felt right to do that. In fact, I could do so much more since I was beginning to feel less like the person I was and much more like the hucow that he showed me I was.

He moved his hands around me and he found my boobs, massaging and fondling them for what felt like an eternity. With his body on top of mine, I could only wonder how much longer I was going to last until I came. After all, my body was already growing warmer and sweat drops were forming on the skin, and I could feel my climax growing in intensity.

Robert continued to knead my breasts for a couple more minutes before moving his hands away, and it happened the moment that I thought I was going to come. Turning my head to look over my shoulder, I asked, "why did you do that? It's so unfair."

"Because, right now, I want to milk you and I don't want you to come so quickly without us first doing something special," he responded and then kissed the nape of my neck, sending shockwaves of pleasure through me.

I even arched my back, something that never happened every time Warren did this to me.

And I couldn't help but wonder where he was.

A few seconds after that, we heard footsteps walking into the room. I turned my head to see who it was and I was hoping that it was Jeremy, but it turned out that he was just Warren.

My pathetic ex. He didn't have anything else to do with me other than how much he wanted to see a better man using me, and he was getting his wish right now.

I chuckled.

What else was I going to do when my ex decided to show up and prove that, in the end, he really was nothing more than an asshole that never deserved me?

"Warren? What do you think you are doing here?" I asked, going straight to the point.

"I was just… Checking to see if you needed anything."

I cackled. I couldn't believe that he came here just to see if I needed something, one of the reasons why I found him to be so pathetic.

Robert looked up and found him. "If you are so intent on helping us, then you can help us by cleaning her milk on the floor."

Warren blinked twice in a row. "You want me to… clean her milk on the floor? But I don't even have a piece of cloth and a floor squeegee."

Robert waved his hand, showing annoyance. "You aren't going to need those things. You can do it with your tongue and lips."

Warren opened and closed his mouth several times in a row and he truly couldn't understand what he should do. The moment that Robert showed he was going to punish him for being so clueless, he rushed to me and positioned himself underneath me.

I knew that he could move fast when he wanted to, but I didn't think that he could humiliate himself even more than he had done several times before in his life.

He met my eyes one more time before putting his tongue out and beginning to lick the milk on the floor. It was already leaking, so there was a sizable pool on the floor.

Despite his thirst, it was still going to take him a while to lick everything off the floor. And for a moment, I couldn't do anything but watch my ex underneath me, his tongue sweeping over the milk pool.

After chuckling again, Robert prodded my pussy with his prick, trying to slide it in. I looked over my shoulder and asked him if he was going to do that right now, and he confirmed it by just easing his dong inside of me, one inch at a time.

Grimacing, I didn't think that it was going to be so painful, to the point where I thought my sex would never be the same after this.

"Oh God, oh God," I mumbled over and over again, and at that moment I had already forgotten that Warren was still licking the milk on the floor.

Was he doing a good job? I didn't know. I couldn't even hear the noise that his tongue was making, swiping on the liquid.

After a while, Robert managed to put himself all the way inside of me, and then he stopped. He didn't do anything, which made me wonder what his plans were now.

"Jesus. It's really so big. I never thought that there was a man so big in the world," I confessed after huffing. Breathing was so difficult now, but it was nothing to worry about.

After looking down, I saw that my ex had almost finished licking the milk on the floor. There wasn't much more left of it on the floorboards, and even though my udders were still leaking more of it, it would take a while until there was another sizable pool on the floor.

"And, right now, I'm going to eat your pussy and take your virginity. You want me to do that, don't you?"

I smiled and confirmed, "it's everything I want, actually. I want you to do that and to show my ex that he could never be the same man you are."

"That I can do," he confirmed before rolling his hips, slowly in the beginning but then picking up the pace a couple of seconds later when he was used to what he was doing. In a few seconds after that, he was doing it at full speed, destroying my sex while slapping his balls against my ass.

We could all hear the slapping sounds echoing in the room and it only added to the feeling that this was the best sex dungeon that ever existed in the world.

I moaned, groaned, and mooed, all the while wondering when he was going to come into my sex. I was fertile and he could get me pregnant by doing this. I was sure that was one of his plans, even.

CHAPTER 5

A few seconds after that, I couldn't hold back the rising orgasm in me, and it was devastating when it happened.

My body shook with everything it had and I thought that I would never recover from such a powerful, shattering experience, one of the reasons why I was hoping that this was going to be it for today and we could relax until we had more energy for another round.

But I didn't know if that was what Robert had in mind, and I wasn't going to risk asking. I wasn't that crazy. The last thing that I wanted to do was to piss him off.

A few seconds after that, I looked down and saw Warren looking back up at me, smiling with some of my milk still on his lips.

He just looked so pathetic it made me wonder how I was able to put up with him for so long.

I moved my hand around his face, saying, "you did a good job cleaning up, but now... Scram. Get out. I don't want to see you around here right now."

He opened his mouth and he was going to say something, but then I put my index finger on it and stopped him. Whatever he had to say to me, I didn't want to hear it.

He stood up in a heartbeat and then disappeared from the room, leaving me alone with Robert, who guffawed.

"You really put him back in his place. That was amazing and funny at the same time," he said before erupting inside of me, shooting rope after rope of his come and filling me up with it. And there was so much of it that some was even dripping out and staining the floor again.

It was a reason to think that maybe I was a little too hasty when I ordered him to go out. He could do another cleanup job, this time focusing on the come that was now pooling on the floor.

But that was something for another time and, right now, I was focusing on gripping Robert's dong inside of me, and it was... Breathtaking.

He stretched my walls to the point that I was certain they would never be the same ever again. I couldn't help but wonder when the baby bump would become noticeable.

But as with so many other things, that was something for another time, and I could only focus on feeling Robert's massive dick inside of me. It almost felt like he wasn't thinking about pulling out anytime soon.

"This is so good," he purred before sliding his hand over my shoulders, focusing on all the pressure points. It was as if he was massaging them.

"I think that you shouldn't pull out. I want you inside of me for the rest of my life," I pleaded, smiling.

But in the meantime, I couldn't help but wonder when he was going to fuck my asshole, too. In fact, my mind was already obsessed over that, one of the reasons why I wanted it to happen right at this moment.

Sometimes, I could be impatient, just like it was happening now.

"Really? That would be so unfair to Jeremy. I'm pretty sure that he is already coming here, after all, and we don't want to disappoint him. He is as entitled to you as I am."

"You're right, but it would be so unfair to me if you pulled out right now. That's why I'm hoping you aren't going to do it. Or, if you do it, I hope that you do it slowly. I don't want it to happen so fast. After all, I'm still getting used to feeling you inside of me, and I'm certain you can understand me."

"I understand you, pretty," he said before gliding over my ass, following its curvature. I wanted him to finger me, but the butt plug was still in there. By now, enough time had already passed to the point that I couldn't even fill it inside of me anymore. It was as if it had always been a part of me. "But Jeremy and I are buddies, and I would never cross him."

I groaned, but couldn't argue. Robert was right about that even if I didn't want to admit it.

A few minutes after that, he began to pull out of me, and he did it quickly, much to my disappointment. Wondering what was going to happen next, I was happily surprised when Jeremy showed up at the door.

Now that I was thinking about it and this thought was popping into my mind, I wondered if Warren could show up here again so that he could finish another cleanup job after these millionaires were done with me.

He was already naked, as he should be. He was ready to get into the fun with Robert, who had already finished pulling out of me, his semen dripping from the slit. Just looking at it, I felt a sliver of thirst in me.

But my attention was quickly returned to the man standing in the doorway, who was already pumping his dick and preparing for this inevitable moment.

"I'm going to fuck you so hard in the ass right now and by the time I'm done with you, you will be begging for more and more. If there is something that all the other members of the Dairy Club think I am, it's how ruthless I can be when I'm in the right mood."

I licked my lips. If he was going to be so ruthless when fucking my ass, then I was already waiting for that to happen.

My body was even begging for that.

CHAPTER 6

It was only a few seconds after that that he went behind me, filling in the gap left by his buddy. I knew that he was going to do that, but I was still surprised by it and for a moment I didn't know how to react.

But the moment that he put his fingers around the loop on the butthole, I knew exactly what to do, and I mooed.

He slid his hand over my shoulder, enjoying the softness of my skin.

"Are you ready for this?" He asked, tugging at the butthole, but without removing it. Not yet, anyway. He was taking his time and, in the meantime, Robert positioned himself in front of me, teasing me with his prick. Licking my lips, I thought about sucking him off right now but only with his permission.

"I am," I responded without having to think too much about it. It was just the right thing to say at the moment, and it put me even more into the right mood than I already was, and I could just imagine him now filling me with his dong.

After that happened, he would shower me with even more pleasure than I could endure, and I wasn't kidding.

"Good. That's exactly the answer I was looking for," he murmured into my ear before pulling the buttplug out one inch at a time. He was taking his time doing that and I loved that about him, one of the reasons why I wanted him stuffing me full with his massive, oversized dong.

And to think that it was going to happen now... I just couldn't wait any longer.

A few seconds after that, the butt plug was out of my asshole. It had come out with an audible pop. I could already feel my walls trying to return to how they were, but they couldn't.

My asshole would never be the same and I wasn't exaggerating.

He slid his finger around my asshole, feeling the ridges. "Jesus, it's really something else, just like Robert here said it was, and I can't wait until I'm inside of it. Fucking an asshole is so much better than eating a pussy, not to mention that Robert was already the first inside of you there, so I want to do something a little bit more different."

I knew what he meant by that and I could only moo when he slid his finger into my hole, widening it a little bit more by pressing his fingers against the walls. I knew he was going to do that, but it still kind of caught me by surprise. I had really thought that he was going to plunge deep inside of me with his shaft.

I was already pleading for that to happen.

I mooed again and he said, "it's so warm and still tight. I'm pretty sure that when I'm inside of you, you will feel more pain than you think possible, and that's putting it mildly."

I knew he was right about that, and my expectations for that inevitable moment were only increasing right now.

Robert, after teasing me that he was going to let me suck him off, slid under me, grabbing both of my boobs. With his hands already massaging and kneading the skin, it took him very little time to show me exactly what he was going to do, and I could only groan when he eased one of my nipples into his hungry mouth.

He slid his tongue around it and continued to do what he was doing for what felt like an eternity, and then he began to suckle on it, drawing out milk. That continued to happen while Jeremy only teased that he was going to eat my rectum, and I could only hope that he wasn't going to take much longer to do that.

A few seconds after that, Jeremy eased his prick inside of me, one inch at a time and I could only curl my toes. The pain was almost intolerable, but I didn't say anything and just decided to bite my bottom lip as much as I could without drawing out blood. I felt that, if that happened, I would be more worried about what was happening to me than I already was.

A few seconds after that, Jeremy was already fully inside of me and I could even feel his balls pressing against my ass. I was still getting used to his size the moment that he started to pound in and out of me, and the most surprising thing about this was that he was at top speed from the get-go.

Moaning and groaning, I could only shut my eyes right now. The best thing about this was that they were both pleasing me from both ends, and they were relentless.

The only thing I did that I thought I wasn't going to was to look to the left when I heard footsteps coming from the door. It was, just like I had thought it was, Warren and he was even already jacking off while watching this development.

It really turned him on, didn't it?

A few moments after that, my body began to shake and I erupted. I was having the best orgasm of my life, and I wasn't exaggerating. A few moments after that, Jeremy erupted inside of me, and even though he wasn't going to knock me up just like his friend did, it was still a moment I would never forget.

I was huffing by the time this was over and he remained inside of me even after he spurted out the last rope of come. In the meantime, Robert emptied my jugs, and I knew that it was going to take a lot of time before they were filled with milk again.

This was such a memorable moment that I didn't want both of them to stop what they were doing. And as if he could read my mind, Jeremy confirmed as he murmured into my ear, "don't worry, pretty. We still have so much energy to burn and we are going to do that with you. We are going to come into your pussy and all your holes several more times, and then we'll show everyone that you are ours."

EPILOGUE

A few moments after that, it was determined that nobody else could enter the Dairy Club. It was an exclusive club that wasn't accepting any more members, and it only filled me with joy that I was one of the few women allowed to be a part of it.

In the meantime, Warren became my servant, and now he had to do everything I wanted. He even had to wear a puppy mask and a tail, all to please me. He had always been a puppy to me, but now it was official and he had to play by my rules even more than before.

That was one of the reasons why I put my legs over his body. He was on all fours before me and I was sitting on the couch. While doing that, I brought up the grape cluster I was holding in my hand, and then I popped one of the grapes into my mouth, savoring it.

"Hmm," I said, enjoying this a lot more than I thought I was going to.

Right after that, Warren said, "I'm so happy that you are enjoying yourself a lot more with those guys. I'm nothing like that, and that's something that I've already grown used to. It's okay, really. Sometimes, a man just has to realize that he is inferior."

I cackled and, while putting another grape into my mouth, I heard footsteps coming into the room and I turned my head to see who it was. I wasn't surprised when I found none other than Jeremy, Robert, and the other members of the club with them.

They were all here, including the other hucows. They were all gazing at my glistening pussy, and I knew that they wanted to do unforgivable things to it, things that we would never be able to erase.

Stacy and Sheryl... They were kind of jealous of me, but they had been in the same situation before, and they knew what it was like to be pampered by these millionaires.

As usual, every time that they were here, they were naked and their shafts were pointing at me. Glancing at them, I licked my lips. I wanted to mouth them for hours on end, and that just might happen now.

"Are you ready for this, Diana?" Jeremy asked, his eyes flashing with evilness. "When we start round two with you, we will pound you until there's nothing left of you, and by the time that we are done, you will be begging for more of it and we will claim you so hard that it will be impossible for you to remain awake. You will most likely pass out and you are okay with that, aren't you?"

And after hearing his words, I could only nod.

Of course I had no problems with that.

The End

Don't forget to read the first two books in the series here:

1. Hucow Flavor: Endlessly Milked by the Billionaire
2. Hollywood Hucow Shared: Cuck's Wife Knocked Up

Thank you for reading this story. Leave your review. Your feedback helps me immensely!

SIMILAR BOOKS

Hucow Flavor: Endlessly Milked by the Billionaire (Dairy Club - 1)

Things have become desperate for Stacy. Fresh out of college and with a mountain of bills to pay, she can't even afford the rent for her rundown apartment. On top of that, she's still undeniably pure, and she has always wanted to lose her V-card. Men just don't seem interested in her, and it doesn't help that she only has eyes for older, experienced guys.

Especially if they are billionaires…

Her mind can't stop obsessing over the ad she's seen in a newspaper. It could save her, but there's a strict catch. She has to offer up her body to the Dairy Club, a group of midlife billionaires with a filthy love for milk. They plan on milking every drop that her curvy body can produce, and even then, it wouldn't be enough to quench their ever-growing thirst.

Days later, Stacy takes the plunge and is dropped off at a sprawling, imposing estate, and what happens from then on will change her completely.

Further reading:

SERIES - Hucow for White Collars

1. Milked by Lawyers
2. Milked by Doctors
3. Milked by Engineers
4. Milked by Directors
5. Milked by Managers

SERIES - Auction Club

1. I'm his Property
2. He Owns Me
3. Billionaire's Fertile Risk
4. Grad Student Fertile Accident
5. Fertile Bimbo Trained
6. Owned for Being Bratty

SERIES - Fertile Only

1. Bumping the Teacher
2. Bumping the Midwife
3. Bumping the Farmhand
4. Bumping the Sinner

SERIES - Hucow for Blue Collars

1. Milked by Plumbers
2. Milked by Firefighters
3. Milked by Policemen
4. Milked by Electricians
5. Milked by Miners

ABOUT THE AUTHOR

Leandra Camilli's obsession? Writing dirty, steamy stories that make her readers drool. She loves her Alpha males, hucows, sissies, and futas. If you're looking for those kinds of books, look no further.

With a cup of coffee on her table and warm socks on, she writes almost every day. Leandra Camilli has featured in several top 100 categories in the store, and she publishes weekly.

Join Leandra Camilli's Facebook group here!